The VIRGINIA Night Before Christmas

E.J. Sullivan

Illustrated by

C.J. Franks

SWEET WATER PRESS

The Virginia Night Before Christmas
© 2005 by Sweetwater Press
Produced by Cliff Road Books

ISBN 1-58173-392-5

Printed in China

The VIRGINIA
Night Before
Christmas

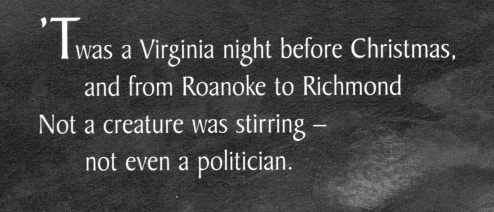

'Twas a Virginia night before Christmas,
   and from Roanoke to Richmond
Not a creature was stirring –
   not even a politician.

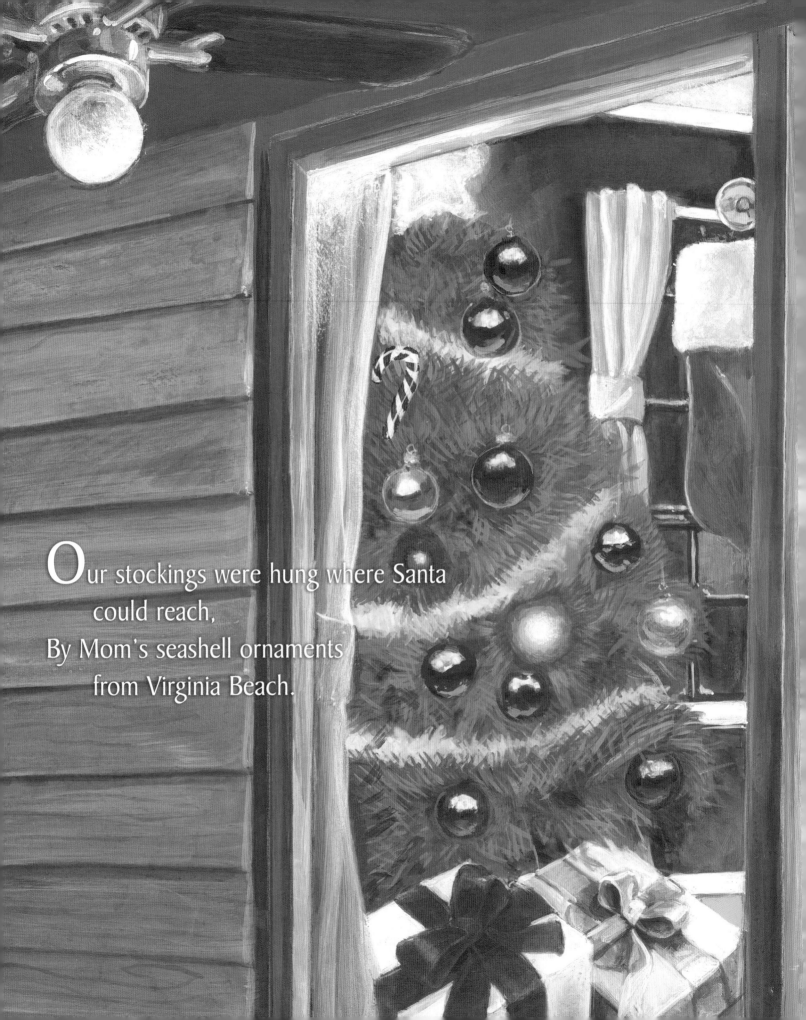

Our stockings were hung where Santa
        could reach,
By Mom's seashell ornaments
        from Virginia Beach.

Baby Sister was snuggled all safe in her bed
With visions of cheerleader stuff in her head.
And me in my Cavaliers jammies, and Luke in his Hokies tee,
Were each of us dreaming of playoff victory.

When out by the gas grill
a sound made me quake –
Like when troopers get behind us
on the interstate!

I sprang to the window and threw
open the shutter,
Armed with Dad's new autographed
Sam Snead putter!

The moon was as bright as that Cracker Barrel store
They put in down the road – it's open all hours!
And then what to my wondering eyes should I spy
But a team of thoroughbred reindeer flying by!

With a little old jockey
so lively 'n' quick,
He coulda won the Triple Crown
any old day in a lick!

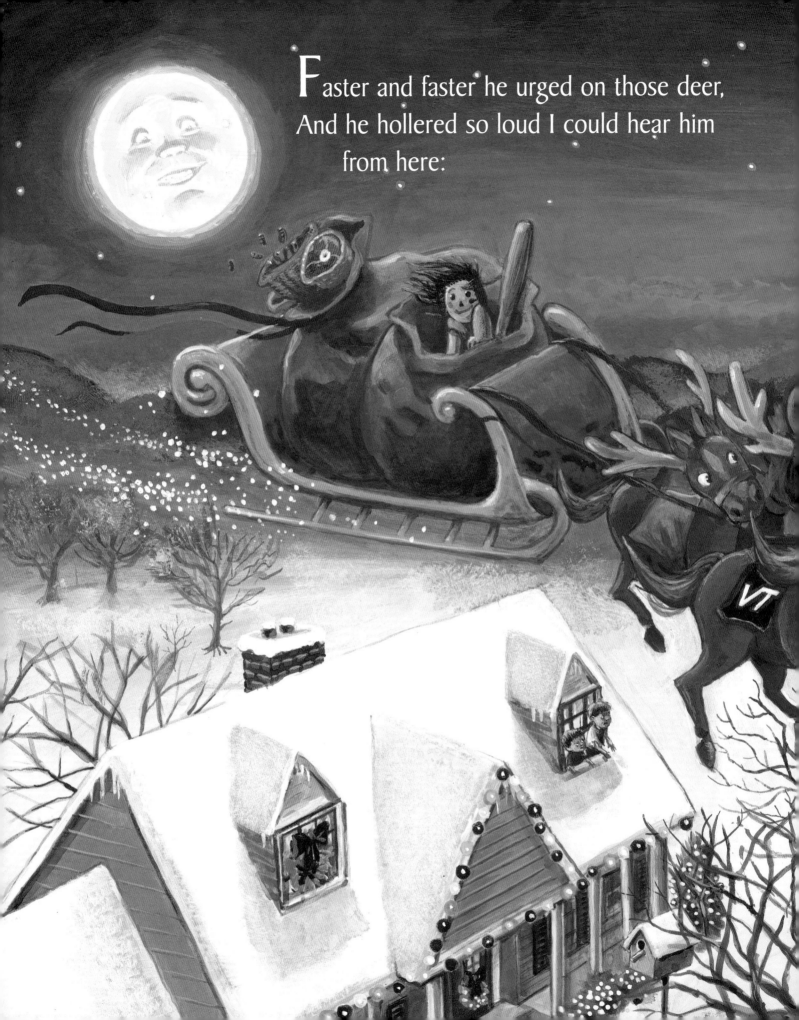

Faster and faster he urged on those deer,
And he hollered so loud I could hear him
from here:

"Get up Washington, Jefferson, Madison, and Harrison!
Go Monroe, Tyler, Taylor, and Wilson!
Around Martinsville Speedway! Over the Blue Ridge soar!
From the roof of Monticello,
        to the Chincoteague shores!"

You know how those re-enactors
get dressed up for their deal
Looking so much like great grampa
you can't tell if it's real?
That's how confused I was when those
thoroughbreds raced by –
Got me so worked up I needed
an RC and Moon Pie!

As I finished my snack I saw
our dogwood tree shake
When the hooves of those reindeer
started to scrape.
I looked up through the limbs
and caught him red-handed –
On our Luray Caverns birdhouse
Santa'd crash landed!

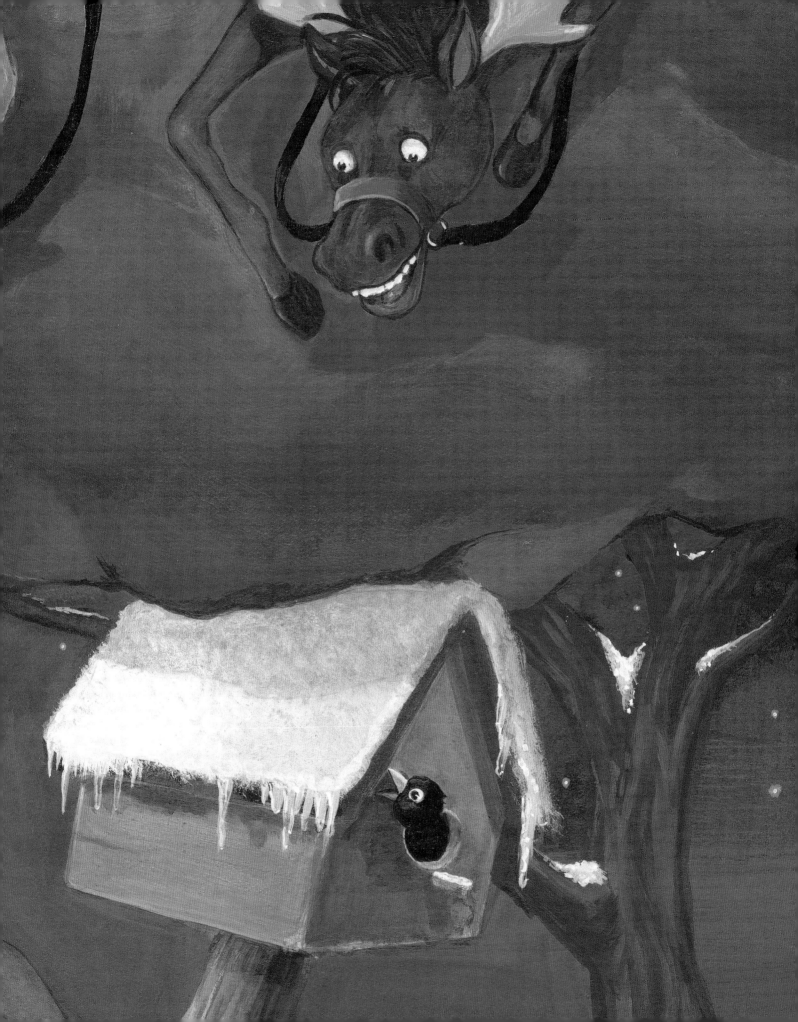

Bless his heart. He looked a lot like General Lee,
With his hair and his beard tangled up in that tree.
Mom's always saying I should help folks who are older
So I helped him get down onto our John Deere mower.

Santa stepped over our dog,
    Stonewall Jackson,
And put peanuts and ham in our stockings
    for snackin'.

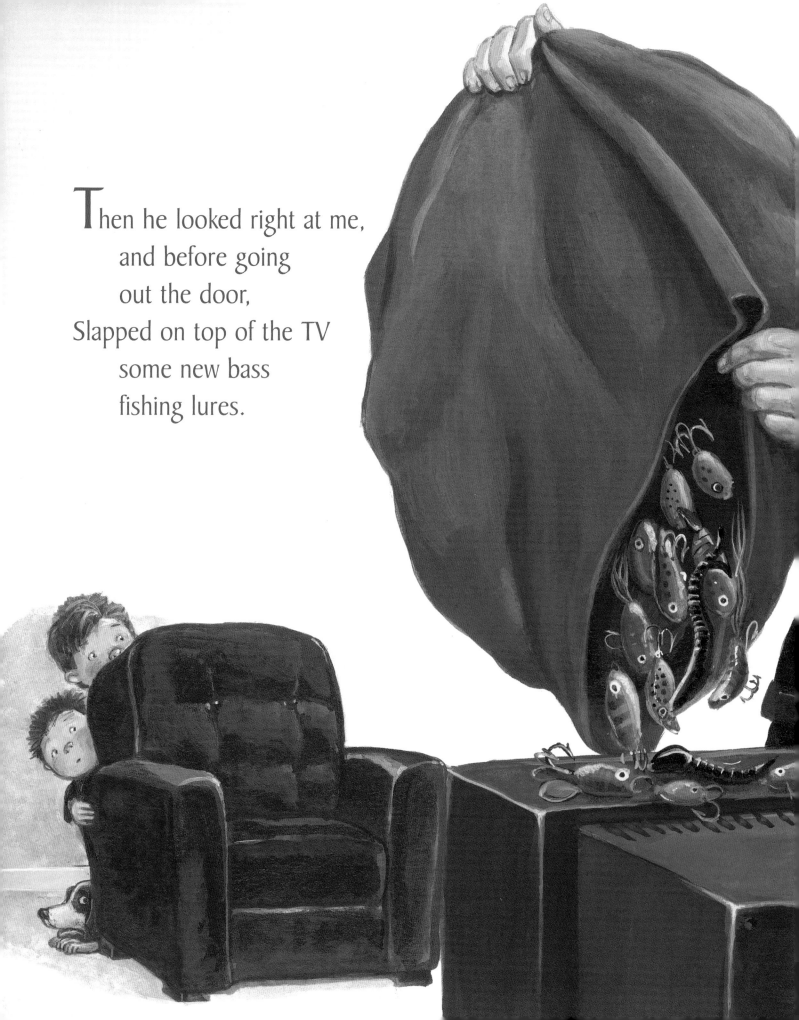

Then he looked right at me,
and before going
out the door,
Slapped on top of the TV
some new bass
fishing lures.

He climbed back in the saddle
and soon he was gone,
All the while telling those deer
to race on.
But I heard him holler out as his
team sped away,

"Merry Christmas, Virginia!
I wish I could stay!"